Dear Divya

Dear Divya

Saira Batasar-Johnie

Dear Divya

The first chapter of this story was published in *Two Times Removed: Anthology of Indo-Caribbean Fiction* (2021)

First Paperback Edition July 2022

Edited by Tiara Jade Chutkhan & Nabeeha Ali
Cover Design by Stephanie Rambharos

ISBN 978-1-7781897-0-8 (Paperback)
ISBN 978-1-7781897-1-5 (ebook)

To my husband Neal for always supporting me in all my dreams,
I would not be here without you.

To my sons, Nekai and Nelin, and my niece Sephira, I wrote this so you
could see yourselves represented in a book. The names from your
culture, the foods you eat, and the stories you will hear.
I love you three to pieces.

To every young brown person who wished they saw themselves in
literature, this is for you.

We are the Gold
Our ancestors were
Promised.
—Anna Chowthi

Contents

Foreword

Growing up, I was never a fan of reading, and I struggled due to my learning disability. I read slowly; I didn't know how to read words and so I avoided it altogether. It wasn't until I started high school that books such as *Go Ask Alice, Memoirs of a Geisha, The Kite Runner*, and *Anne Frank's Diary* piqued my interest in reading.

The one thing always missing for me was that I never saw myself represented in the books I read. There weren't girls and boys who looked like me, who had names like myself or my family members, who spoke in the dialect my parents did, or were Caribbean. I always wanted to see myself represented in a book or a show, but it never happened. To this day, it is still seldom seen to have an Indo-Caribbean person as the main character.

I am writing this series for all the young, Indo-Caribbean people who love to read and want to feel seen and heard. The people who would like to see themselves reflected in a character. At the same time, I am writing this series to educate the next generation about where Indo-Caribbean people within the diaspora come from and how our parents migrated to a different country to start a new life and give their families better opportunities. I want to highlight their struggles in daily life, as well as the identity issues that many of us experience while growing up in a predominantly white country, but also break those barriers and the stigmas that are rooted within us and the generations before.

I don't want us to lose ourselves and assimilate into the general public. I love being Indo-Caribbean. I love my culture, my food, the music, the accent, the language, and our history. These are the core values I want to continue to pass down to my children, and therefore I hope these books will continue to support that.

I wrote this for our daughters,

I wrote this for our sons,

I wrote this for the next generation,

And I will continue to write for them.

Our voices were silenced,

No more will we be quiet.

For our ancestors,

For our past,

For our future,

We will no longer be silent.

Recap

Waking up on Saturday morning, Anjali recognized her parents listening to Ingrid and her father on channel 3 (whom the community all knew as "Uncle") updating the Indian & Indo-Caribbean community about upcoming events and news on the TV.

The smell of curry loomed through Anjali's bedroom. The soon-to-be 14-year-old was up late talking to her cyberspace friends on Habbo Hotel and MSN, something which her digital immigrant parents had no idea. Their young, innocent daughter could meet strangers and talk to them about anything under the sun.

"Anjali, wake up! Half da day done finish pikney," Anjali's mom yelled from the kitchen.

Anjali's mother, Seeta, was an older woman who had immigrated to Canada in her twenties during the Burnham period in Guyana. Seeta had become an illegal refugee living in hiding and working cash jobs; she couldn't go back home because it wasn't safe. A neighbour had found out about Seeta's situation and reported her. She had to move quickly, and with the help of her friends who knew a single Indian man looking for a wife, she was able to get married to the stranger and receive her papers to stay in Canada. Anjali's mother was number three of eight siblings; her childhood was very different compared to that of her daughters being raised one of ten children and very poor in Guyana. She had a hard exterior and was very strict with her daughters, resulting in two rebellious teenagers. Seeta did not want her girls in the kitchen, she wanted them in their books, but the two girls had other plans. The girls didn't see their father much as he would work 12-16 hour days running the family business. Seeta was often left to raise them alone.

Anjali got up and cleaned her recent nose piercing. She felt so proud of her new piercing, as her older sister Amara had also gotten hers done right before she started high school. It was almost like a rite of passage for her. Anjali saw that her mother had left a basket of laundry to hang out. She popped the latest Aaliyah CD into her discman. "Rock the Boat" blared through her ears as she left her room. She ignored what her mother was saying and walked out of the house with the basket.

As she hung out the laundry, she practiced her dance moves and wondered if she would kiss a boy this year; if someone would notice her since she had lost weight and developed her new curves. She wondered if the girls that bullied her for smelling like curry, being hairy, and having big hair would now admire her defined eyebrows and want to be her friend. Would she fit into high school the way Amara did? She wondered if she would meet other girls who looked like her. Anjali lay in her hammock in the backyard wondering. "One in a Million" started playing as she thought about how she had watched her sister sneak around behind her parents' back with boys. She wondered if she would too.

***

It was the first week of high school and all Anjali could think about were her outfits. She wore big silver hoops, a tight black t-shirt, blue skinny jeans, and her new Baby Phat black and white sneakers.

She reminded herself of what Amara had said to her: "Don't talk to me if you see me, just keep walking." Of course, that hurt Anjali, but she was used to Amara being mean to her sometimes and then being best of friends with her other times. That was easy since they were dropped off at different times. Anjali's mom dropped her off; Amara had first-period spare, so they didn't come to school together.

Seeta spoke up before Anjali left the car, "Anjali, don't talk to no boys, focus on your schoolwork, yuh hearin me?"

Anjali looked at her mom while rolling her eyes and responded, "Yes Ma."

She left the car and her mother waited until Anjali
entered the school before she drove away.

When Anjali opened the doors to her high school, all she
could see were BOYS. So many boys, Anjali felt her cheeks
blush. Then she saw her best friend Kristen and smiled instantly.
Kristen had pale skin with freckles; she had been Anjali's friend
since the first day of middle school. They'd both never been part
of the cool crowds. Anjali didn't have any Caribbean or Indian
friends because there weren't any besides the one other Trini
boy who purposely ignored Anjali because she smelled like curry
and wore her hair in a long, long braid throughout middle
school. Anjali was set on creating a new image for herself in
high school; she was done being "Curry Girl" and wanted to
embrace her newfound curves, nose piercing, and curly hair. To
her, that meant no more long plait braid. She was done being
bullied. Students from four different schools were at this high
school, there were bound to be new Brown or Black students, she
hoped, people that didn't know her.

Kristen and Anjali compared their schedules and quickly
realized they had no classes together. This was devastating.
Whom was Anjali going to sit with? Talk with? She felt worried
and nervous. They entered the cafeteria for grade 9 orientation
and everyone from middle school looked at her as if she was a
new person. She noticed people from other schools she had
played against in basketball tournaments as she and Kristen
walked to an empty pair of chairs. There was a group of Brown

and Black girls that looked her up and down, but she brushed it off.

Jamie walked up to Kristen and kissed her on the cheek. She longed for a boyfriend. Kristen had a boyfriend since grade 7 and Anjali had constantly third-wheeled with them throughout grade 8.

She wondered what Divya would have thought about first-day jitters, it was something they used to talk about all the time.

No one wanted to date the Brown girl who had braces, was chubby, had thick, frizzy, hair always braided, and ate unusual food for lunch. Anjali struggled with her appearance; she knew she didn't look like her peers with their blonde or brown straight hair, different-coloured eyes, and skinny bodies. She wanted to look like them, but her mother forbade her from dyeing her hair and getting coloured contacts.

She listened to the principal's announcement and then they dispersed to their classes. Kristen told her where they would meet for lunch, hugged her, and off she went. Anjali checked her schedule and started walking to room 108 – geography. She had to walk through "The Circle" where all the cool kids were; she saw Amara, who was in grade 12 now, with her glowing dark brown skin and freshly straightened hair. Anjali's mom wouldn't let Anjali use a straightener; she was scared it would damage her curls. Her mother didn't know how to maintain curly hair—

besides putting coconut oil in it—which often led to big frizzy hair.

Amara was being hugged by a tall Black guy who looked like he played some type of sport, given all the guys around him wearing jerseys and the girls who looked like they were already in college. Anjali and Amara's eyes locked.

Amara grabbed her and said, "Damian wanted me to introduce you to everyone. So, everyone, this is my little sister, Anjali. Don't let shit happen to her. Okay, bye."

Anjali waved awkwardly and started walking. Damian ran up to her, "Hey, I know your sister is weird about you being here, but if you need anything, please don't hesitate to ask. High school can be really shitty."

"Okay, cool," Anjali said and smiled.

Thoughts ran through her head all at once. Oh my God, my sister is dating a Black guy. Oh my God, my sister is popular. Oh my God, does this mean I am popular? Oh my God, Mom and Dad can never find out, we would both be dead! How is my straight A sister so cool? She was floored at what she had just experienced.

Anjali made it to her classroom, walked in, and a boy named Kevin who teased her almost every day in middle school looked at her and said, "Oh, hey look, it's Curry Girl!"

Everyone giggled. Anjali told herself she wasn't going to put up with this bullshit anymore, so she lashed back.

"Go f*ck yourself Kevin since no other niner will."

"Go to the office!" screamed the teacher.

Anjali walked to the office. She couldn't believe she'd ended up there on the first day of school. She felt amazing, like a rush, it also felt like she was going to get a brutal cutass when she got home. She sat there waiting for the principal to call her in. Suspended for two days. Her mother was on the way to pick her up.

Anjali waited outside. She saw Amara and told her what happened. Amara told Damian. They said they would deal with Kevin.

At that moment, Anjali saw him…

His brown skin.

His light brown eyes.

His spiky hair.

He had a lineup around his chin connecting to his moustache.

His baggy pants.

He had a baggy white t-shirt on.

His plump lips.

A Guyana flag hung from his back pocket and he rocked a Jansport backpack.

He wore fresh white Air Force 1s.

He had his earbuds around his neck with a soca mix blaring from it.

He. Was. So. Hot.

He shook hands with Damian. Damian looked at Anjali and said, "Anjali, this is Naraine."

Before she could respond, Amara disappeared, and their mom pulled up to the front of the school. Anjali had never been suspended before; she was in for an earful from her mother.

*She got into the car and her mother blazed her all the way home with a lot of "Wah de m*dda ass", "How yuh so schupid", "Amara has never been suspended", and "Wait, you just wait. You are grounded, I takin that blasted Discman. Yuh tink you can ignore me? Hmm you can listen to some bhajans and maybe God will heal you". Her mother went on, but Anjali tuned her out because all she could think about was Naraine and if he even noticed her. She wondered why her sister was being so nice to her. So many things were happening on the first day of school.*

Anjali got home and went to her room. She gave up her precious Discman. She laid in her bed; her heart thumping so quickly as thoughts about this boy that had infiltrated her mind made her feel hot and flushed in her face.

She opened her journal.

Dear Divya,

Today would have been our first day of school together. You would have loved it; there were boys everywhere— short and tall, fat and skinny, in all different colours, not like middle school. There were even Brown boys! I know, I was like thank goodness. Finally, mans that don't go to temple that I can chat to. Oh, yeah, I also got suspended and my mom is losing her shit. I wonder if Dad will even care or notice I exist. He has been extremely distant since you…

*Remember Kevin? Yeah, I swore at him and told him to go f*ck himself. He's so stupid, he called me Curry Girl as per usual. I have no time for bullying in grade 9— not having it. You wouldn't believe this either— Amara was nice to me at school. Remember she was always like, "Don't talk to me in front of my friends" or would use us to get out of the house and go hang with her friends. Now she's a completely changed person. I wonder if she and I will become friends… I miss when we were younger, and she was so nice. When she started high school, she became this weird, "I'm too cool for you person" AND she's dating a Black guy! I think she's badass considering we aren't allowed to date, much less date a Black person and the most popular guy in school… so cool. I won't say that to her though…unless she's nice to me.*

And then there was Naraine, who I looked like a total jackass in front of today. He was this beautiful 5'11" body of gorgeousness. His eyes! His skin (no pimples fyi.. I hope I don't get any this year)! Damian (Amara's man) was introducing me to him and my mom totally cock-blocked me when she started honking the horn. I wonder if he will notice me again, or if he will talk to me the next time, I see him. I wonder what cologne he was wearing. I secretly want to go to the drug store and buy it because, girl, it smelled so good— like dreamy, good— like Nelly take off all your clothes. LOL, I am being so silly. I hear my mom calling me to clean since there is no homework.

I miss you.

Love,

Anju

Returning to School

The radio alarm goes off…

> *"You are now listening to Kiss 92.5…*
>
> *What's my mother***n' name?*
>
> *R-U-L-E*
>
> *Blowin' back on this Mary…"*

I hit snooze and rolled over. My mother enters my room and opens the blinds.

"Get yuh backside up! Go bade and get ready fuh school."

Mom made fry bake, saltfish, and tomato for breakfast which stunk up the whole room and my clothes for school. If it's not curry, I smell like, it's my dad's favourite food.

My mother drove me to school. It was silent in the car, which wasn't typical. She even turned the radio off, didn't play her regular bhajans. Silent treatment was her speciality sometimes. I felt as if she was upset with me, but without the noise that she typically makes. I wished Amara was in the car to break the silence.

She parked and we went into the school. The principal wanted to meet with mom before I was allowed to go back to class. I sat and waited outside of the office while they talked. You would think meetings that are about me would include me. I tried to listen to their conversation

"Mr. Beckham, please you must forgive my daughter, she had a very difficult 8th-grade year," my mom pleaded.

"Mrs. Singh, I completely understand. You have provided me with my star student Amara, so I will not keep this on her record, but we must think of a reasonable consequence for her behaviour. Swearing in class is not tolerated," Mr. Beckham responded.

"Hmm, I do see you have a garden."

I plugged in my earphones, Amara let me borrow her iPod, and began to tune them out. The outcome— "Anjali, please go to class!" Huh? I'm confused. Why no attendance or behaviour contract? Whatever, I'm not complaining. My mother looked at me with those mom eyes and she spoke loud and clear with them. She managed to keep the suspension off my record. Instead, I got a month of after school detention.

I walked into geography and looked across the room. Kevin had a black eye and a mashed-up lip. Oh man, did I do that to him? He kept his head down. No one else said a word to me either. I saw another Brown girl sitting by herself, so I sat beside her. She was listening to her iPod; I could hear a *Mortor mix* coming from her ears. Oh my God! Could she be Caribbean too?

The girl had pin-straight hair that looked super silky. She was wearing black leggings and a big white T-shirt with the front tucked in. You could tell her boobs had come in because her shirt was sticking out significantly— something I didn't have as yet. She had a gold chain with her name on it, big hoop gold earrings, shiny, shiny lips, and black Air Force 1s.

She looked at me. "Hey, I'm Shantelle, Suriya's sister. I think our sisters hang out together. She told me to look out for you."

"I'm Anjali, Amara's sister. That's cool."

"Wanna listen? I just got these songs this weekend at the flea market. It's the latest Chutney/Soca mixes," Shantelle said.

"Yeah, totally!"

We sat there listening to music until class started. During the work period, Shantelle and I got to know each other, made fun of our sisters, and made plans to hang out at lunch. She seemed really cool.

Shantelle mentioned how my sister is so lucky she gets to date Damian in the most sarcastic tone and rolled her eyes as if I didn't know what she meant. It is so disgusting and disappointing that she would think race would be an issue, like hello it is 2004, who cares? The underhand comments were so rude. It didn't sit well with me, but I didn't know how to address it.

"Man, yuh sistah is a rebel. My sister told me that your mom is the temple going, bhajan listening, prayers for everything type of mom. Amara looking for licks when yuh muddah find out about Damian."

I stayed quiet.

***

It was lunch. Shantelle and I met at the square. Kristen walked by.

"Anju let's go; Lauren found a really cool spot to eat our lunch. Did you bring the rodi *(roti)* and curry beans *(same curry)* your mom made last night?

I pulled her aside.

"Kristen, I'm going to eat lunch with a couple of new people I met in the first period. They are Amara's friends' younger sibs."

She looked at me with her big brown eyes. Her smile faded. I knew I hurt her feelings and I felt so bad.

"No problem, Anjali. You do you," Kristen responded and walked away.

"Yo Anjali, you ready?" Shantelle said very loudly.

We walked off school property and I felt like a rebel. My mom told me never to leave school. As she'd say, "You nah know wah man can tek you and hol yuh up." But I was with a group. Shantelle introduced me to her other friends. Everyone was either Brown or Black. Stacy Ann was from Jamaica, she immigrated from there when she was seven. Marcus was Afro and Indo-Guyanese, Sunita was from Trinidad, and Avinash was Trinidadian and Guyanese. For once I felt like I belonged. Some of these new friends had older siblings that knew Amara, and some were just Shantelle's friends.

We went to the local 7-Eleven plaza where there was a 2for1 pizza place. We all pooled our money and bought a pizza for lunch. *I'm so going to have to finish my roti and same curry before I go home or my mother will murder me for wasting food,* I thought to myself.

We grabbed a table and started eating. Just as I took the first bite of my pizza, Amara and her friends walked in. Amara looked at me instantly and called me outside to talk.

"Listen, you need to be careful with Shantelle. She may seem nice, but she's not."

"But she knew so much about you from her sister. There was this instant connection."

"I understand, but I've been burned by her sister. I'll explain later at home."

Damian came and put his arm around Amara.

They are so cute, I thought to myself.

I couldn't shake off Amara's words. I'd just made my first friend and now I had to be careful. It doesn't sound fair; just because she made bad choices with friends doesn't mean I have to listen to her. Maybe Shantelle is different now? After all, she did introduce me to all of her friends. Also, why is Amara being so nice to me? She fully well halla up at me at home to not talk to her and now, home girl wants to be my friend. Schupes.

My mind felt conflicted. I went back to the table and finished my slice of pizza.

***

Dear Divya,

You wouldn't believe what happened today! I met other Brown people, like Brown girls and guys that are West Indian! How cool is that? They eat the same food we eat, and they smell like curry too (well, their backpacks do).

I met this girl named Shantelle today. She seems really cool. We listened to music and even hung out during lunch. Her sister Suriya and Amara are the same age and they're friends, so I guess it only makes sense for us to be friends, right? We even went to the plaza today and ate pizza. My mother would kill me if she knew I didn't eat my butter dish container of roti and same curry.

I also kinda ditched Kristen today, which wasn't cool, but I really wanted to hang out with these new people. Yuh aunty also got my suspension off my record, but I do have detention after school starting tomorrow for a whole month, smh.

Anyhow, Amara came and warned me about Shantelle, but I don't get her. One minute she's nice and the next she's like one thorn in my backside. I can't read her; we just haven't been the same since you...

I wish you were here. I wish I could share all these things with you. I've stopped crying in the shower as much, but when I think about you, I get really sad. Dad is still never home, and Aunty Deepa hasn't called. I hear mom leaving messages asking her to call back or come home, but we haven't heard from her.

Sigh.

Until next time,

Anju

Detention

I have never been in detention before. All of this was new to me and completely out of my character. What can I say? I'm enjoying the new me. Although, I'm terrified of going to Mr. Beckham, the principal's office, and "making Amara look bad". I wanted to create an identity for myself instead of just being "Amara's little sister" and living in her shadow.

I entered the principal's office. He directed me to the backroom, and I sat there waiting.

Naraine and another boy from their crew, Jamie, walked in. They sat in two different spots. Naraine sat closest to me. I could smell his cologne.

"Eh yo, look little 'Mara is here," said Jamie.

I sank into my chair feeling my face and body get hot. If I were a white girl, my face would be red— the perks of having brown skin.

Naraine gave me the head nod "sup" and smiled.

I stayed quiet, not knowing what to say. The sky, um, nothing? Um, I love you.

"Just here," I said.

Mr. Beckham came in and explained we have detention for one hour. He gave us a piece of paper and told us to write out what we did, why we did it, and why we won't do it again. No talking. He left.

Naraine took out his iPod and I heard Rupee start playing. I could hear "Tempted to Touch" and boy, if he only knew how tempted I was to touch.

"Anjali, right?" He asked, looking at me.

"Yeah."

"Why are you here? Your sister is such a goodie goodie."

"Um, I… yelled at a boy and swore in class."

"Look at you, badass."

"Oh, the kid Damian and Kamal dealt with?" asked Jamie.

"I guess." I started writing.

My heart had started beating 100 miles a minute.

"So why are you here?" I asked Naraine.

He looked up and smirked. "Wouldn't you like to know?"

"Well, yeah. That's why I'm asking."

What the hell? Was he flirting with me? What am I doing? I need to just stop talking now.

"I'm late every morning. I can't be bothered to wake up on time."

"Yeah, because he's too busy talking to Chanel at night," giggled Jamie.

"Bro, I told you I'm done with that. Drop it."

I stayed quiet. I looked at him when his head was down. His spiky hair was hard as a rock, probably from half a bottle of gel, with a fresh line up. He looked so delicious, I just wanted to smell him… Ugh, what is wrong with me?

"Is something on my face?"

Shit, he caught me watching him.

"Uh no, no, I was just looking for the time."

"It's 3:38. We are almost done."

"Okay, thanks."

I wonder who Chanel is. Is she my sister's friend? There go my chances with him and his beautiful self, ugh.

It was 4 p.m., and detention was now over. Mr. Beckham came and collected our sheets.

"Now, Miss Singh, your mother and I worked out a deal. You will be spending time cleaning up our community garden and helping in the library for the next month after school," Mr. Beckham said in his stern teacher voice.

"No problem," I replied. *Dah lady knows I hate yard wuk.*

I left detention and sat on a bench waiting for Amara to finish a Student Council meeting.

Naraine and Jamie walked out of the office.

"Yo Jay, I'll meet you at the plaza."

Naraine walked over to me and sat down.

I could feel my heart racing again. I sucked in my tummy hoping I didn't look fat, as my mother had called me fattish this morning. I started playing with my fingers. Why did he come to sit with me?

"So, are you cleaning the garden tomorrow?" Naraine asked.

"Yeah, I guess."

"Cool, cool. I'll be there this week. Do you have Facebook?"

"Yeah." *No, I really don't.*

"Add me up."

"Okay."

"Cool, so I'll see you tomorrow, lil 'Mara."

"It's Anjali, and yup," I responded, annoyed.

"Haha, she sticks up for herself, I like dah. I gotta bounce, but I'll check you later. Don't forget to add me." Naraine walked away as Amara walked towards me.

"Why were you talking to Naraine?" Amara asked, very concerned.

"It was nothing."

"You don't know how these mans are, so please don't be stupid. Let's go, mom is waiting for us."

***

Dear Divya,

Girl, you would not believe what happened today! I talked to Naraine. We had detention together and gyal, my heart felt like it was going to come out meh body. Like, I wanted to drop down and faint. He is so hot and dreamy! With his spikey hair and facial hair, ahh. He asked me if I had Facebook. I came home and made an account really quick while I had time on the computer before my mother came and tek away cords. You know how nutso she is. Remember that time she took my friggin mouse? Jeeze dah lady head nah good.

Amara told me to be careful, but she still hasn't really talked to me. Ugh, I wonder if she knows Chanel. I wonder if she is pretty, or what grade she is in. Chanel, I am guessing, is Naraine's ex-girl.

I stood in front of the mirror poking my belly today. Mom told me I'm looking real fattish. Since I got my period, my body is different. It's so heavy and so uncomfortable. I hope I get boobs soon.

Anyhow, until tomorrow.
Anju

Amara & Damian

Amara was my parents' first born child; three years older than me. I'm pretty sure she is their golden child; gets straight As in school, plays the piano and harmonium, and sings at the temple. All the aunties love her. She is like the poster child for a perfect daughter. Daddy-Ji takes her to the store more than I go and he's taken her to India. Then there's me who has never been to India and I cannot speak Hindi for the life of me. But I can understand everything, it's like a secret power.

I feel like my parents invested so much time into Amara and kinda forgot about me, or just expected me to do everything Amara did, but that didn't work out too well for them. I don't like the harmonium, I love playing the tabla. I don't sing, my voice is nothing compared to hers. I'm not a straight-A student either. The only thing Amara and I really have in common is our love for classical Indian dancing. We've both attended Aunty Indra's Bharatanatyam dance school. As sisters, we were one of the best dance teams. I loved dancing with Amara. It was our outlet from the world around us. When Divya was around, it was the three of us against the world; it was so much fun. Dancing for me and Amara hasn't been the same, but we continue to push through since Mom loves it.

***

It had been in the middle of the second term in middle school; Amara was called down to the office. A new student had been enrolled into her class, and being the model student that she was, the principal relied on her to support new students and help them adjust. This new student in particular was Damian. When Amara stepped into the office and saw Damian, their eyes locked immediately. Damian with his curly black hair in an Afro hairstyle, baggy jeans and a big t-shirt, his smooth dark-brown complexion. It was an instant little crush; her heart beating fast and mouth running dry.

"Hi, I'm Am..mmara," she stuttered.

So many thoughts ran through her mind. She was young. Who knew they would end up where they are now?

***

Damian and his family moved to Toronto, Ontario from Vancouver, British Columbia. His paternal grandparents had immigrated to Canada from Jamaica, his grandfather a mechanic and grandmother a nurse. They worked hard to provide for their children, experiencing poor work environments and racism. Damian's dad followed in his father's footsteps and became a mechanic, later evolving into an engineer. He didn't know much about his mother's side other than her family was Scotian— from Nova Scotia— they were considered Black Scotians. His mother was an educator, she taught primary school and has been a principal for the past 15 years at different elementary schools. Both of his parents strived to provide a good life for their three children. Damian's older brother had gone to the Caribbean for medical school; it was their grandmother's dream to become a doctor, so Damian's older brother Dwayne was determined to do just that in her honour. Damian's sister Danielle had received a full scholarship to the University of Toronto to study Pharmacology and this was why they made the big move— to be close to their only daughter.

Damian wasn't sure what he wanted to do; he loved taking things apart and putting them back together with his dad. Something broken always intrigued his mind to try and fix it. That's what attracted Amara to him— his brain and how smart he was.

They were both sports lovers; Amara played soccer and volleyball, and Damian played hockey and soccer. He also enjoyed participating in student groups which stoked Amara's heart even more. They were born leaders, meant to run the school together.

The friendship between the two of them evolved as they started high school. Both became very popular: Damian had become the school's youngest star athlete playing hockey and Amara had joined every student leadership extracurricular. Amara planned their first school dance in grade 9, and Damian had built up the courage to ask her to be his date. She said yes.

The two of them shared their first dance to a Boys II Men song and then their first kiss. Amara was terrified, but she had also never felt like this for anyone. She took a leap. They've been together ever since.

Her only fear was her mother finding out, as boys were completely prohibited until she was 30. As her mother liked to remind her, "books before man".

Gyal, Bye!

"Yoo pass the shovel," Naraine shouted at me.

I felt butterflies every time he spoke to me; I hope he didn't see me blush.

"When I used to live with my Aja, he would make me clean up the garden with him every weekend"

"That's sweet, I'm sure he enjoyed the company."

We sat together and took a break from cleaning the entire school garden. This was our last day doing this.

"So, you going to miss me after spending your after-school time with me?" Naraine asked.

The butterflies started.

"Uhh no, I'll be fine. If you miss me, you can always message me on MSN." I tried to be flirty, not sure how it went.

We both laughed.

"I like your chats, Miss Singh, you got jokes."

We talked about the most random things. He would tell me about the Raptors and the upcoming season, I would nod my head and act like I knew what he was talking about. Sometimes we would talk about our families. From what it sounded like, it's just him and his mom; he doesn't really talk about his dad. I let him do a lot of the talking.

I wonder if we'll continue chatting each other up.

I wonder if he likes me.

***

It had been weeks since community service in the garden was completed. Naraine and I had grown closer. We started messaging each other on Facebook and then added each other on MSN. We stayed up until all hours of the night messaging each other. My favourite game to play with him was 21 questions.

It was a different story at school, though. He acted like I didn't exist. I started to wonder if something was wrong with me. Why was I a secret? Why was he treating me like this? There were only a few moments when we would share a smile or make eye contact with each other. I loved talking to him, and we even spoke on the phone a few times. He had a cellphone, but I didn't, so I would call him on the landline when everyone else was sleeping.

My friendships with my new friends also grew stronger. I hung out with them every lunch, during breaks, and even sometimes on weekends if my mom let me go out with Amara. I stopped hanging out with Kristen or made excuses as to why I couldn't chill with her. Shantelle did not like Kristen, and she made it clear that I wasn't allowed to hang out with her. I had to make a choice, a hard choice. Kristen and I had been friends since grade 5. When Kristen first came to the school, Divya and I were her first friends, and it stayed that way until now.

Shantelle was really controlling; she was very vocal about who I could and couldn't talk to, what clothes to wear, what clothes not to wear, how to do my hair, what earrings to wear, etc. The other girls didn't seem to mind, so I just went with it. It was my first time having friends who looked like me and I didn't want to ruin it. Amara hated it, but why would I listen to my big sister? The only secret I kept from everyone was that I was talking to Naraine.

Kristen approached me while I was in the library at lunch and asked me to talk. She was alone.

"Hey Anju, can we talk?"

I looked around to see if anyone could see us.

"Sure, let's go to the bags." We walked to the bean bag area in a corner of the library, behind the bookshelves.

I had allowed our friendship to crumble. We'd become so distant from each other because I was hanging out with my new friends and didn't really want to stay connected to my old friends.

Kristen began to cry.

"Anju, I miss you. Why have you been ignoring me? What is happening with us? We've been best friends for years and now just because Shantelle is cool or something you want to hang out with her all the time? Jamie cheated on me and I tried to call you. You haven't returned any of my calls. Why are you doing this?"

I froze, not knowing how to respond. Shantelle told me to cut Kristen off or I couldn't hang out with her crew anymore. Instead, I just chose to distance myself, so I didn't have to have that hard conversation. Now it's happening. Cut the friend that was in my life when I had to deal with life-changing events. Cut the friend who slept over, ate all the curries and roti, bake and saltfish, and Caribbean food your heart desired without a complaint of it being too spicy. She loved my family and my culture. Kristen was one of the only white girls that would come to my house and not say it smelled like curry. But none of that mattered anymore, I had new friends, people that looked like me and talked like me.

"Are you done?" I looked at her with a blank stare.

Kristen looked at me, we stared at each other and sat in silence.

"So, I guess this is it. I guess our friendship means nothing to you. You know, I wonder what Divya would say or what she would even think about the cold person you've become. You are such a bit——-"

I cut her off. "Don't you dare speak her name. We are done."

Kristen gathered her things, got up, and walked away. She threw a photo of her, Divya and I from grade 7 leadership camp back at me.

I sat there.

I took a deep breath in and sighed, tears rolled down my cheeks as I looked out the window.

***

Shantelle started sleeping over at my house on weekends; we became inseparable. Where there was Shantelle, there was me and when we were apart everyone would ask where the next one was. We were batty and bench.

I felt like I finally had a best friend, someone who looked like me, ate my food, and listened to the same music. Someone I could mock my mother's accent with and laugh until our tummies hurt. There were days that I didn't think about Divya and the pain slowly disappeared.

It also felt weird as I slowly started to become more popular. I joined several different student groups at school and started making friends outside of my core group of friends. Shantelle wasn't too happy about that. She started to become possessive of me. She wanted me to message her on MSN as soon as I got home. She made me feel bad about having other friends, so she made me hang out with her every lunch. I started to feel suffocated, but I assumed this was how besties were.

Shantelle would sometimes make passive-aggressive comments about my appearance such as, "No man gah like yuh with yuh bushy hair", and "Girl, you know I jokin". I would brush it off, but those comments hurt my feelings. She always agreed with my mom.

Shantelle started dating a grade 11 boy at the Catholic school down the street. His name was Marcus and he was half Jamaican, half Portuguese with gorgeous green eyes. Her time began to get busy with him and she was less in my business 24/7.

I finally felt comfortable enough to tell her about Naraine. One weekend, Shantelle slept over. She had just gotten into a huge fight with Marcus over him having friends that are girls and she was not okay with it. She was crying in my bed, but she noticed me on MSN smiling.

"Who are you talking to?" Shantelle asked in an annoyed tone.

I froze. Naraine and I had kept this a secret from everyone because he was worried about what Amara and Damian would think given he is a part of their friend group and they don't really date younger siblings (he had finally told me why he was shady at school).

"Umm, okay. I'm going to tell you, but you cannot tell a soul. You promise?"

"Sure."

"So, since detention a few months ago, Naraine and I have sort of been talking… ish."

"What do you mean talking ish?"

"Umm, like we stay up at night on the phone and he writes me notes and puts them in my locker type talking. I've been crushing on him since September."

Shantelle looked at me as if she had just found out I kissed Marcus or did something wrong.

"Okay cool, now can we get back to my life and my drama?" Shantelle said.

Something didn't feel right after sharing the news with her. Your best friend is supposed to be happy for you and excited about your crush. Shantelle was just annoyed with me. Did I make a mistake by telling her? The nervous butterflies in my tummy started.

I spent the rest of Saturday and Sunday catering to Shantelle's needs since she slept over. Kristen never made me feel like this: belittled, worried about what would happen if I didn't message her. Kristen just didn't understand the culture, but she was a great friend.

At that moment, I missed my old friend.

Betrayal

It was the Monday after I had told Shantelle about Naraine. I felt a sort of relief that, finally, someone knew. I got to the square where everyone usually hung out and saw Shantelle flirting with Naraine. Everyone was looking at me and whispering, then looking at Naraine.

I froze. My heart sank.

We had been talking for months and he was finally starting to be seen with me at school.

Shantelle touched his arm, stroked his hair, giggled while they spoke, and stood really, really close to him. Naraine stood there just holding the bottom of the straps on his backpack.

Shantelle had everything I didn't have— a perfect body with boobs something I barely have, silky straight hair, lips perfectly glossed, hoop earrings, and a small waistline.

Why would she do this? Did she tell everyone?

Shantelle saw me and quickly backed away. Naraine saw me and looked embarrassed, his eyes dropped to the floor. I quickly walked to Sunita and Avinash who were hugged up in a corner, grabbed Sunita, and dragged her to the washroom.

It had gotten out that I liked Naraine, but I had only told Shantelle. Sunita was telling me what happened, but I couldn't listen to her. Shantelle must have told everyone. I started pacing in the washroom.

"Why, why would anyone do this? It's been months of us being so close! Shantelle is supposed to be my friend, friends don't do this!"

Sunita and I had developed a really good friendship, but because she and Avinash were dating, they were always together, and we didn't hang out as often.

"Umm Anju, she told everyone you are obsessed with him, and that you have a shrine at your house all about him," Sunita told me.

"What? Oh my God, my life is over. Why would she do this? I thought we were friends. I thought we connected. Why, why, why?" I locked myself in a stall.

Amara came into the washroom. Sunita tried to get me out, but she couldn't. Amara told Sunita it was okay to leave as the bell rang for class.

"Go away Mara," I said with my voice trembling as I cried.

There was a brief pause of silence.

"Listen, I'm your sister and I care about you. What Shantelle is doing is not cool and I'm here for you," Amara responded with a kind voice.

"You don't get it. You are perfect; your hair, your skin, your brains, your body, everything about you is perfect. I'm nothing. I can't compete with these other girls. I'm not like you."

Silence.

"Anjali you're right, you aren't like me. In fact, we are completely different. But that's what makes you unique— your thick, curly, bushy hair, your beautiful dark brown skin. Girl, you have a booty for days. You have big, beautiful, almond brown eyes, and you are so smart. I can't begin to tell you how proud I am of you for joining the leadership team and student council— and putting yourself out there when I know how hard this past year has been for you."

Silence.

I haven't heard my sister be this nice to me in a long time. It made me even more emotional, and I started crying more. My self-esteem had dropped since Shantelle always agreed with my mom about me being fat and my hair being a big beast that needed to be tamed. Along with making small comments about other parts of my appearance as well. I never realized how hurtful it was until now.

"I'm sorry. This is so dumb. I'm crying over a boy. I'm so stupid."

"So Naraine, eh. Hmm, he's something, but you know what Mom would say— I send yuh to school to study books, nah man," Amara said, mocking their mother's accent.

We laughed.

I came out of the washroom stall, my freshly applied mascara running down my cheeks. Amara wiped my tears and hugged me.

"I love you Anju, and I'm sorry I haven't been there for you. I warned you about Shantelle. Her sister is no different, but that's a story for a different day."

I embraced my sister; she smelled like Baby Phat pink perfume and coconut oil with a hint of the saltfish and tomato my mom made that morning.

"We have the dance to focus on. Stay clear of Shantelle for a bit, and just focus on your other friends and school."

I told her what went down with Kristen, how controlling Shantelle has been, and how deep down I felt like I was suffocating.

We hadn't bonded like this in what felt like years. Our mother has five sisters and three brothers, but they were always fighting, or one sister wasn't talking to another sister. I thought we would end up like that, like our mom and her sisters. But now I can hope that things will be different.

I took a deep breath and left the washroom.

Saira Batasar-Johnie

New Crew?

A couple of weeks had passed since the whole square ordeal. I hadn't spoken to Shantelle and noticed her and Naraine spending more time together. Despite this, Marcus was still picking her up after school. I can't believe her. I can't believe Naraine.

Snake.

I started hanging out with a few other people I had met in my other classes. One was Priya Malhorta, an Indian girl. Her parents were from India, and she was born in Toronto. Priya had never heard of a Guyanese and Indian mix before; she thought it was cool but was kind of puzzled that I didn't speak Hindi. We had applied math and academic English together and after English was lunch. I had shared what happened with Shantelle and so Priya invited me to hang out with her and her friends during lunchtime when I wasn't planning the dance or going to leadership or GSA meetings with Jacob.

Jacob was my childhood bestie, but we kinda grew apart when we went to middle school. We still loved each other tons, but just had different friend groups.

At first, I felt relieved I had new friends to hang out with, but then I started feeling kind of awkward around them when they were all speaking Hindi. They didn't know that I could understand them. Moments like these I wished my dad was around more to teach me instead of learning from watching Indian movies.

Priya introduced me to Simran, Kurti, Naval and Jasvinder. They were all so nice to me, aside from a comment that was made about my Guyanese family being "lost Indians" by Simran's brother who was in grade 11. I didn't understand what he meant. My mom always told me our family were farmers back home.

One lunch we all sat outside to eat by the rocks on school property. I had brought dahl and rice with fried okra and aloo for lunch. Simran had roti with aloo curry, Kurti had biryani, Priya had dahl and rice with curry Chana. I didn't feel different eating my food with so many different smells and deliciousness; it felt homely.

A group of white kids walked past us.

"Go back to India."

"Pakis."

They walked away laughing.

I looked at the girls, but they all had their heads down.

"Shut up, losers!" I yelled back.

I had no idea who those boys were, but it wasn't cool speaking to us that way.

"It happens all the time, you just get used to it," Simran said.

"Oh, I know, I had it bad in middle school with the white kids. They constantly bullied me for my brown skin and smelling like curry," I shared.

"We all smell like curry," giggled Kurti.

We all laughed.

***

Joining the leadership student group and student council was huge for me. This wasn't my thing. My things were standing up against bullies, the art club, the dance team, and the Gay Straight Alliance, or GSA, student group at school. I had joined because my friend Jacob had asked me to go to the first GSA meeting with him. My mom always says "gyal is fuh man and man is fuh gyal". I was questioning my sexuality but wasn't sure how to explore it—if I was even allowed to, Jacob was my only friend who knew one of my biggest secrets.

Jacob and I had both been bullied by the same people in middle school for being different. I had a fire inside of me after being bullied constantly for three years. I wanted to use my voice and stop being this shy, quiet girl people could pick on. I joined GSA because Amara wanted me to join the leadership student group and student council. I tried to balance with the other student groups, but the commitments were difficult to keep up with. Between lunch meetings, and school planning committee meetings, I felt stretched thin, but also busy. Busy enough to keep my mind off certain things, like Shantelle and Naraine.

Shantelle hadn't spoken a word to me since the whole ordeal went down, but she told Sunita she felt really bad and wanted to make up with me. I also missed my friends and wasn't sure if I could continue hanging out with Priya and her friends. Even though they were really nice, I felt out of place because I couldn't bond with them when it came to the language.

In the leadership group, I had been planning the dance, which was exciting because I got to work with Amara. The relationship between Amara and I became kinder and softer. Amara stopped being so mean and cold to me, she actually started to be nice. I wasn't sure if this was because she had found out she got into McMaster University and was leaving, or if she genuinely wanted to be there for me and be my big sister again.

We worked on the decor for the gym together. The theme was Under the Sea, and I got help from the art club to create some pieces for the wall. While I would work on my art, my mind couldn't help but wander. I wondered if Naraine would talk to me again. I thought about talking to Shantelle again. What would it look like— would we be friends? Could I trust her again? I felt someone looking at me. I looked up.

At the gym door, Shantelle stood there watching me. She walked toward me.

"Can we talk?"

"Sure…"

Amara came into the gym just then and saw us talking.

"Listen Anjali, I am really sorry. Please let's just talk this out."

"I just— I just don't know if I can trust you again…"

"Anjali, mom is waiting for us. Let's go," Amara interrupted.

"I'll message you on MSN," Shantelle said as I walked away.

When I got home, I didn't turn my computer on. I felt so much heaviness. I looked at my journal and began to write.

Dear Divya,

I totally wish you were with me. I made another new friend. Her name is Priya and she's Indian! Like your type of Indian. She introduced me to her friends who were all Indian and spoke Hindi or Punjabi. You would have been my translator since you spoke both languages. They had never met a Guyanese person before— or someone who was half Indian. When I explained that Guyanese people are from India, one of the boys said, "Oh yeah, your people are lost Indians". I didn't know what that meant so I just stayed quiet and talked to someone else. I'm pretty sure he was trying to be rude or make a joke. I don't know if I will hang out with them again, but Priya seems to really like me, so maybe. We'll see.

Ugh, I still have to tell you about Kristen, but that will be for another time. You won't be happy with me. I can see your face right now making your angry eyes with your unibrow you were so proud of. I miss that angry face.

Oh, you would be so happy to know that Amara got into McMaster University, the life science program on a full scholarship. Now Mom doesn't have to work her weekend job anymore or as much as she has. We will see what happens when I have to go to school.

Another thing that happened today is that Shantelle and I talked. I know what you're thinking, but really, she's not all that bad. You totally wouldn't like her, but she's really cool and she's West Indian. I've never had a West Indian best friend before.

Anyhow, she apologized for what went down and apparently, she isn't into Naraine. Hard to believe, but I forgave her.

I really hope things will be different. The dance is coming up soon and I hope Naraine and I talk before then.

Okay, the lady is callin' me to come wash dishes! It felt good talking to you.

Miss you always gyal,

Anju

Flashback

It was Sunday. I could smell my mom making chicken curry, dahl, rice and buss up shot roti as she would every weekend Daddy-Ji was home. The aroma made its way through the house, forcing me to get out of bed and open my window.

It was raining.

I laid on the floor of my room. I could hear my parents arguing, that's all they ever did these days.

"Yuh is never home! Meh, hav fah raise dese two pikney by meh self."

That was the last thing I heard.

I got my headphones for my iPod; "Closer" by Goapele played on repeat.

I closed my eyes.

"Divya! Anjali! Amara! Come and eat please!" Poowah Deepa yelled from the kitchen.

She had just finished cooking aloo curry with chana and garlic naan— our favourite. The sounds of Lata Mangeshkar were coming from her radio in the kitchen as she hummed every tune.

I looked at Divya. As always, it was a race to the kitchen. I won, but she totally let me. We both sandwiched her mom. I loved Poowah Deepa; she was the best and way nicer than my mom.

We ate so much food that our bellies were going to bust. Poowah Deepa was one of the best cooks ever. She made the most delicious food all the time. Hanging out with her was simple and peaceful.

Poowah Deepa had beautiful long black hair; she would wear it in two braids and then wrap it up in a bun so intricately. She had fair brown skin with hazel eyes; Divya got her complexion from her, but not her eyes. I loved watching her in the kitchen; it was as if she was creating a masterpiece every time she was in there, like a tabla player and his tabla creating music. Whenever she and my mom would cook together, my mom would teach her all the Caribbean dishes and they would compare them to the dishes from India. They were best friends. She made my mom a better person.

Poowah Deepa and Divya moved in with us when her father moved back to India because Poowah had decided it was time to leave him. He had been physically abusing her for years and had started verbally abusing Divya. Poowah had finally told her brother, Abhinav (my dad), and they moved in with us. Uncle moved away. This is what I gathered from eavesdropping on conversations. Divya struggled with her dad leaving her, but often kept it to herself. I knew she struggled because she wore her feelings on her face.

"Girls, do you want more? Amara, are you coming? Beti the food will get cold."

We would always hug up and watch an Indian movie with her on Sundays. The Omni channel always had an Indian movie showing. This week it was Devdas; I love me anything Shah Rukh Khan. Amara and Divya loved Salman Khan; he was meh if you ask me

We all sat on one couch and watched the movie. Poowah would play with our hair and rub our backs. She was so warm and cuddly; I loved everything about her.

I opened my eyes. Tears ran down my cheeks.

"Anjali, gyal dah stairs nah go sweep itself. Amara, find yuh tail and hang out the laundry downstairs. Why I must repeat myself, ah don know. Like meh geh two hard ears pikney."

"Five minutes Ma." I responded, then shut my door.

I wiped my tears and looked at my journal. I realized I hadn't written to Divya as much with Shantelle being in my life.

Dear Divya,

Life isn't how we planned grade 9 to be. I went from being not cool, to cool for two seconds, and now I don't know where I stand. Life would be so different if you were here. You wouldn't be happy. Kristen and I aren't friends anymore. I chose Shantelle over her, all because she was Brown. We are still trying to make the friendship work, although now I have some serious trust issues.

And Naraine, don't get me started. Dah gyal outed me to everyone at school telling the people dem my business, ugh. Now we'll probably never talk again. We were secretly talking behind everyone's back and I confided in Shantelle. Yuh know, I think she wants him, but that's so stupid because she was dating dis man name Marcus from the Catholic school down the road. Anyhow, yeah, he totally thinks I'm some kind of stalker now. Ugh. It makes me sad, sad that he wouldn't just talk to me and find out whats up.

You would be proud about this. I've joined the student council and leadership. We are currently working on the end of the year dance and prom. Amara has been super nice to me. It's weird and fun all at the same time. It's like how it was when you were around. She and her man are so cute; I hope Mom accepts their relationship. Daddy-Ji is still MIA all the time. He just doesn't know how to cope since everything happened to you...

I miss you and I miss your mom. I hear my mom calling her saying, "Deepa gyal call me back nah man", in the voicemails she often leaves.

I have to go sweep the stairs now. I'll keep you posted on the Naraine situation—hopefully we will talk soon. I do miss his chats. He's so dreamy.

Love always,

Anju

Dollah Wine

A couple of weeks had passed; the dance was finally here. Shantelle and I had made up. It was becoming too difficult for everyone to pick sides, so I accepted Shantelle's apology for what she did and her promise that she wouldn't do it again. I forgave her and we went on our merry way. Besides, Shantelle said all she and Naraine would talk about was me. How true that is I'm not sure, but it doesn't explain why he hasn't spoken to me. Although I do catch him looking at me from time to time.

I knew, however, that I needed to be guarded to some degree, but I also wanted a best friend. I wanted that friend group, so I swallowed my pride and became best friends again with Shantelle.

We organized with Sunita what we would wear to the dance. My mom let me sleep over at Shantelle's house that night. On my first sleepover, my mom had no idea what was going to happen with the girls, otherwise, it would have been a huge no-no. Since Amara was sleeping at Leandra's, I was allowed to.

I brought three outfits just in case we changed our minds; none of Shantelle's pants would fit me because my batty was so big, but we shared tops. I wore high-rise black skinny jeans with my white converse and a pink top. Shantelle gave me a push-up bra and just like that I had new boobs! Shantelle straightened my hair which almost took two hours with the size of my head. I put on some eyeliner and glitter eyeshadow, finishing the look with brown lip gloss that tasted like coffee. I was ready. Shantelle wore blue skinny jeans with a white crop top; the school dress code was not in effect for this dance so crop tops were allowed. Shantelle's make-up was similar to mine, and she did her hair half up, half down with two strings in her face for bangs.

I had to leave before her to help set up, so I bought Shantelle's ticket. I told her to come to the front at 7 p.m. and her ticket would be there.

I wondered if Naraine would show up. We had been a bit weird since everything went down a couple of months ago. We had a period where we didn't talk and then randomly he messaged me on MSN. He didn't apologize for anything, more just started talking about randomness, I guess that was his way of smoothing things over. No idea. I hadn't been doing ticket sales and I didn't want to ask him up front if he was going.

As I was walking to the school, I saw Damian and the boys at the park just chillin'. Naraine was there. I waved at Damian and continued walking.

"Weyyyy! Little 'Mara looks like a snack."

"Naraine if you don't get that, I will."

The boys were yelling at me, making me walk faster. I heard Damian yelling at them and then one of the guys said "ouch", so I assumed he hurt them in some way. That made me smile.

"Anjali, wait up."

Oh my Gosh, that was Naraine's voice.

"I really have to get to the school to help set up."

I turned around, my hands in the pockets of my hoodie and there he was; wearing a big, white shirt, with his drawstring Nike bag and baggy jeans, hair perfectly gelled, lips perfectly moistened.

I melted internally once again.

"So imma reach the dance tonight, just because you're organizing it."

He flirted. What should I do? I froze while a million things at once flew through my mind. This was the first time he'd spoken to me in person in a while.

"Cool. I really gotta go, Naraine. I'm already late."

"Okay, no worries. I just wanted to say you look really pretty and I hope you can save me a dance."

He grabbed my hands, pulled me in close, and kissed me on the forehead.

I froze. It was like a magical moment in time, although I could smell the weed on him. This was new, not sure how to feel about this. But then he kissed me on my forehead! A KISS with those lips!

He started walking away, turned back and yelled, "I like your curls better by the way!"

This would be the last time I ever straightened my hair!

I couldn't believe what had just happened. The boys howled as I continued walking.

I got to the gymnasium, saw Mara, and immediately told her what just happened. Amara smiled.

"So, I didn't want to tell you, but Naraine asked Damian if he could ask you out tonight."

"Seriously, Mara!"

"Well, yeah, you know Damian is protecting you like a hawk and he nearly beat the shit out of Naraine after everything went down with Shantelle. I still don't understand why you are friends with that girl again, but we won't go there."

"Ladies, you are not here to mingle. Can you please put these decorations up?" Ms. Santos yelled at us.

I couldn't believe what had happened. Still, in disbelief, I felt over the moon. I couldn't believe what was going to happen tonight. I had never danced with a boy before. What if he wants to grind? How do you grind? What is grinding? I needed

Shantelle and Sunita. I just had to remind myself it's like dancing from Save the Last Dance— I could do it.

Oh gwadddd. 7 p.m. couldn't come fast enough!

***

"Differences" by Ginuwine came on. It was a big song.

I just finished my shift at the snack table and walked into the gym. Everyone was coupled up. Damian and Amara, Sunita and Avi, and Shantelle and Shaun, her new flavour of the month. I couldn't find Naraine. I stood up against the wall. I guess it wasn't happening after all. Then he walked into the gym, he looked around and our eyes locked. He walked towards me. The butterflies in my tummy began fluttering. Oh, gash.

He took my hand and pulled me close to him.

"May I have this dance?" he whispered in my ear.

I smiled. "Yes."

He took my hand and walked me to a spot on the dance floor. He pulled me in close and I put my hands around his neck; his hands were on my lower back, the perfect gentleman.

He whispered the song lyrics in my ear,

"My whole life has changed,

since you came in,

I knew right then

you were that special one...."

I melted. Our eyes locked.

And then... it was going to happen.

He closed his eyes.

I closed mine.

Our lips met.

It felt like butterflies throughout my entire body.

His lips were so soft and plump, he definitely must have put on some lip balm before this. He pulled away and kissed me on my forehead.

We continued to dance. I smelled his shirt— freshly sprayed Adidas cologne. I totally bought the correct one from Shoppers Drug Mart. Note to self— never tell him I bought his cologne; he's totally going to think I'm a stalker, but he just smells so good.

It felt as though we were the only ones on the dance floor. The song ended. The DJ mixed in "No Letting Go" by Wayne Wonder; this was such a big chune. He turned me around and hugged me from behind and slowly backed me up against a wall. Alright, this was it; I had practiced with Shantelle and Sunita. I could do this grinding thing we'd seen in movies.

But we didn't dance.

He just held me in his arms, sang the song to me, and kissed my cheek, our bodies close together, but nothing more.

"So does this mean you'll go out with me?"

"Umm… I think so."

"Oh, you think so?"

I giggled

"Yes, I'll go out with you, Naraine."

He hugged me tighter.

The dance ended. Naraine and Shaun walked Shantelle and I home. Her mom was waiting for us in the living room, and Suriya trailed behind us. We said goodbye to the boys and went inside. Naraine gave me an extra tight hug, and a forehead kiss. I loved it; it made me feel so special.

We made popcorn and gushed all about the boys! I still couldn't believe what happened— actually happened.

Shantelle went to shower, and my mind wandered. I thought about Divya and how I would have loved to share this experience with her. She totally would have thought Naraine was cute, but I think she would've liked this guy named Prashant in grade 10; he is her type. My eyes watered thinking about how Divya would never get to experience this.

"Anjali, the shower is free!"

First Date

I couldn't believe Naraine had asked me out on a date. So many thoughts, so little time. What would I wear? What would I tell my mom? Will Mara help me? I had to figure this out, I really wanted this date to happen. The movie Hostel had just come out and everyone organized to go see it on Friday. A scary movie; I hated scary movies, but for some reason everyone loved them. I was more of a rom-com type of girl, with a little bit of action and mystery.

***

Amara told Mom that she and I were going to the movies with a group of friends. I was allowed out as long as I swept the floor and did the dishes. Easy peasy.

I watched Amara get ready. I still had no idea what I was going to wear. She put a soca mix on Youtube while she did her hair and make-up. She didn't need much; her skin was perfect. She did not go through a pimple stage in high school. She wore sparkly eye shadow, liquid eyeliner, and mascara with some shiny, shiny lip gloss.

"Here, wear this."

Amara took out a pair of black, skinny jeans from my closet and a blue Guess T-shirt from hers.

"Thanks, but that still leaves my hair, and I don't know how-to put-on make-up. Shantelle did my make-up for the dance."

"Well, you have natural beauty, but here I'll do your eyes for you, and you can wear your lip gloss. Leave your hair as is just add some water to spruce up your curls."

I changed and sat on the bed; in moments like these, I enjoyed having a big sister.

"Okay, I'm going to do your liquid eyeliner on your top eyelid; hold still."

"Okay."

"Stop laughing."

"I can't."

"Anju, the liquid is going to go everywhere."

"I can't stop laughing."

Both of us burst out in laughter and we had no idea why. After five minutes of giggling, we stopped. She managed to do my top eyeliner and she showed me how to do my bottom eyeliner.

"All done! You look so cute!"

"Let's go. Ma, can you drop us at the movies?"

"Wah all yuh think? I is a taxi cab?… Schups."

***

Amara and I got to the movies; she told mom she would call when the movie was over. Once we went inside, we saw everyone. Shantelle was with Shawn. Her older sister, Suriya, was there with her boyfriend, Carlos; he was in college and had green eyes and tan brown skin. So dreamy.

Naraine walked over to me with a smile on his face.

"You look pretty."

I'm pretty sure if I were a white girl, I would have been a billion shades of red.

"Thanks, you look pretty too…I mean handsome …hot …..uhhh…"

Naraine laughed.

"Chill. I bought you your ticket, do you want some popcorn?"

"I have money for my ticket here."

"Keep your money."

"Sure, I'd like some popcorn."

Everyone stood in line for popcorn coupled up; it was pretty much a couples' date night.

Naraine put his arm around me as we waited.

"Do you like scary movies?"

"Uhh…Nope."

"Don't worry, you can hold my hand."

Little did he know the last scary movie I watched led to me sleeping with my mom and Amara for weeks. I really hope this movie isn't that scary.

We got our seats in the middle right side of the theatre. Everyone sat in the same area. This was my first time going to the movies with a boy. I always saw people with their boyfriends, but now I'm that person with a boy that's a friend (not sure if he is my boyfriend). I was sitting with a boy, instead of my friends.

The movie began. I sat with my legs crossed and hands crossed. My palms were so sweaty from being nervous; I hope he didn't want to hold my hand. He's going to think I'm totally weird.

Naraine started yawning and slowly put his arm around me. Thank goodness no hands. I leaned in closer to him.

I tried my hardest not to scream or shriek during the scary parts. I totally covered my eyes while he laughed. It was nice to be with him. I felt safe, and at the same time, had butterflies in my tummy the whole movie.

It ended and we all headed to the arcade. Amara called our mom and told her to pick us up in half an hour so that we have time to play a few games. Everyone split up to play games. I saw a photo booth.

"Oh! Let's go take pictures."

"Nah, I'm not a picture type of guy."

"Please, for me. I really want to…." I said turning on my puppy dog face.

"Okay, fine."

We sat in the booth and put our $4.00 in; we got four poses.

Pose one: We both looked at the camera and smiled.

Pose two: We both made a silly face.

Pose three: He kissed me on the cheek.

Pose four: He turned my face and we kissed on the lips.

It was like time had frozen us at that moment. He made me feel like my heart was going to burst out of my chest and explode as if there were butterflies everywhere on my body.

"Yo, are you guys done?"

A quick reality check for me, as we were still at the movies not in Anjali lala land.

Damian and Amara were waiting.

"Aww, look at these photos. They're so cute," Amara gushed.

"Which photo do you want?"

"Hmm, I like this one and this one."

Of course, he chose the silly faces where I look like a goof and the one of him kissing me, skinning my teeth so big. Lawd faddah help me.

We played a round of air hockey. I kicked his butt and it was time to go. I hugged him and smelled him. He smelled so good. He gave me a kiss on the forehead.

"I'll see you on MSN tonight?"

"Yup, for sure!"

"Cool."

The girls walked away together and left the boys in the arcade as my mom was driving everyone home.

My first date. I had a date. I couldn't stop thinking about every moment we shared and now I have photos of us. *Lawd where will I hide this so meh muddah nah go see it.*

When we got home, I showered and logged on to the computer. I left Naraine an offline msg that I was going to sleep early. Hopefully, he got it.

I climbed into bed with Amara because I was not sleeping by myself after watching that schupidness.

Our favourite thing to do when we were little was pretend to put make-up on each other's faces while we talked. I loved the relationship we had; it felt like old times. It's hard to believe she won't be here when I start grade 10.

We talked about the night and fell asleep holding hands. Amara listened as I gushed about Naraine. She reminded me of my worth and gave me the protective big sister talk about dating boys and being careful. She told me about how she and Damian started dating, how he treats her and how respectful he is. I listened and took it all in. I think a part of her is sad she won't be here next year.

I am grateful we are where we are.

I love my sister, I will miss her.

Senior Prom

The day was finally here! We had literally been planning prom since October; it was like planning a wedding. I am so ready for when that time comes now.

I watched my sister get ready for her prom. We had gone prom dress shopping at Le Chateau. She saved a good amount to be able to buy a dress. It was silk material with string as sleeves and a dip in the middle that showed some cleavage. It was long down to her ankles with a long slit to her mid-thigh. Mom was not pleased.

"Why don't you just wear a saree nah. Yuh wan wear a piece ah cloth to dis ting." She said, kissing her teeth and rolling her eyes.

But she had no say; Amara was buying it with her money that she saved working part-time at McDonald's and teaching piano.

The dress was a royal red, absolutely stunning on her beautiful dark brown skin with a pair of red stiletto heels. She was totally going to win prom queen. Our cousin Savita came over to do Amara's hair and make-up. They let me watch each piece going through the curling iron and then being dropped; her straight silky hair became luscious curls. Amara always loved my curly hair, and I always loved her straight hair; any event we had, she always curled her hair for it. Savita did a smokey eye on Amara and painted her lips with red glossy lipstick. Her new stud nose ring sparkled. She looked perfect. My sister was gorgeous; she looked like an Indian Barbie doll. It sucked that Dad missed all of our important events, but Mom took a million photos on the new digital camera she got for her birthday.

Mom dropped Amara at Alyssa's house, one of her friends who had organized the limo for them, and she dropped me at the hall since I was volunteering to help.

"Anjali, who is that black bai matching Amara?"

I froze.

"Uh, I don't know her friends; we don't share friends Mom, that's weird."

I heard my mom mumble, "Mhmm."

She dropped me at the hall.

"Ah go pick you up at 10 pm. Must tell your sister."

"Okay, Mom."

I was at the front table. I took everyone's tickets. Amara walked in with her crew. She looked stunning, literally glowing.

I hope I look like her when I'm in grade 12. Damian had his arm around her, looking all handsome. He had bought her a beautiful corsage to wear on her wrist. Amara saw me and pulled me aside.

"Hey, did you say anything to Mom about Damian?"

"Uhh no, are you crazy? She did ask me who is de bai that is matching you."

"I think Aunty Patsy told her; she saw me and Damian a couple of weeks ago, but I pushed him away. I prayed she didn't see us."

"Okay, well, she wanted me to tell you she's coming at 10 to pick me up."

"Just don't say anything."

"Umm yeah, obviously not."

Amara took me back to the table.

The night went on. I helped Ms. Highgate with tallying the votes for prom king and queen. Everyone knew it was going to be Amara and Damian. They were the sweetheart couple at school.

"Well Anjali, it looks like your sister and Damian stole all the votes."

"That's amazing, she totally deserves it."

I watched as they announced it. There was Amara's perfect smile with her sash and crown and Damian; everyone cheered for them.

I lost track of the time. It was 10:10 p.m. when I saw my mom walk through the door. She watched as Damian kissed my sister on the forehead. Chills went down my back.

"Hey Mom, let's go! Sorry, I didn't realize the time."

She stood there frozen, watching as if she had seen a ghost.

I grabbed her hand before Amara could see her.

She was quiet the whole way home.

Leandra's dad was dropping Amara home from Alyssa's house. My mom said no to the after-prom party, so Amara didn't get to experience that. When we got home, I went to my room and my mom stayed in the kitchen.

I stayed awake. I couldn't sleep. I couldn't warn Amara since I didn't have a phone to text her. I called Savita and asked her to text Amara and let her know Mom saw her dancing with Damian and saw the forehead kiss.

I laid in bed worried about what was going to happen to Amara. We weren't allowed to date. No boys, especially Black boys. Those were the rules— only school work. I was terrified.

***

I stayed up all evening in my room waiting for Mara to come home.

She walked in the door. It was midnight. My mom was sitting at the kitchen table.

"Amara, come and sit down. We mus talk."

"Hi, Mommy! Guess what? I won prom queen, and everyone loved my dress."

"Mhmm. Amara, who is the Black bai that was kissing you today?"

Amara went silent.

I heard talking. I got up and slowly tippy-toed out of my room.

"Amara answa me now."

Amara stayed quiet.

"Amara, Aunty Patsy called yesterday to tell me she saw my Amara, in de road with some man hugging and holding hands. I assume it was the boy kissin' up your forehead today?"

Silence.

"Meh nah kno how much times meh gah fah tell yuh girls don't study man, study your books. As both of you is hard ears. You want to parade like a little hoe on de road with a man— a Black man?! I told you about my sister Guytri! How she ran away with a Muslim man and me faddah was waiting for she. I told yuh rass to this day meh nah hear from she. And how my cousin Parbati leave the house with a Black man in Guyana? My faddah nah let any of us talk to she again. You just don't know what happen back in the day. Yuh want man? Yuh is 17 years old. Why yuh need man for Amara?"

Amara started crying.

"Oh yuh want cry now? Yuh wan go open yuh blasted legs and now yuh wan cry."

"We haven't even had se——-

I left my room and started walking towards the kitchen and listened. I couldn't keep quiet anymore.

"Mom! Stop it! We aren't in Guyana, this is Canada. This isn't the 1970s, it's the 2000s. Stop treating us like this. There is no reason for you to be talking to Amara like this; she is not a hoe and she is not doing anything wrong!"

My mom got up with rage in her eyes and grabbed me by my hair. She pulled me down to the ground and started slapping me. I felt my eyes fill with tears.

"Oh, yuh have mout? Let me show you wah mout go get yuh."

I tried to defend myself. I put my arms out and tried to block the hits. How is this lady hand so hard?

I started crying and screaming for her to stop it.

Amara got up and tried to pull Mom off me, but she laid into her as well. She grabbed Amara's hair and started slapping her repeatedly over and over. I tried to intervene, but my mom's hand was so hard.

"Yuh go call dah bai right now and break up this nonsense yuh have going on. YUH HEARIN MEH?!"

The door opened. Daddy-Ji came home.

"What is going on here?"

Amara ran to our dad and started hugging him and crying. A cut above her eye was bleeding; her make-up was ruined and running down her face. Her dress was ripped.

I sat on the floor, crying, and my mom stood up.

"Yuh big daughtah want to tek man— a Black bai. She wan pick up and disgrace this family name."

My dad looked at Amara.

"Kaala, beti?"

"Haan, but Daddy-Ji, it's Damian. You know Damian, I tell you about him all the time. It's the same boy who is going to become an engineer. He got into the University of Toronto. He isn't a bad boy Daddy-Ji. She would just never understand."

My mom froze. How could Amara tell our father and not her?

"It's okay beti, go wash up and go to sleep. We will talk about this in the morning."

Amara picked me up and we went to the washroom, but we could still hear everything.

"How dare you lay a hand on the girls—"

"Yuh muddah ass man, how yuh go mek me look so schupid in front dem pikney? Yuh is not here to mine dem. Yuh want go work 12 days a week. I have to take care of these girls. I haf fah mek sure dem do good."

"You have no right to hit them. You don't even know this boy. What if he is a nice boy from a nice family? Do you not trust our daughter to make good decisions? Do you not think our daughter who got a full scholarship to McMaster University is smart enough to make a decision about a boy? No matter what the colour of skin he may be."

They continued to argue.

"Are you forgetting Seeta, how my family treated me for marrying you? What nasty things they said because you were Guyanese and not from India? Are you forgetting that Deepa was the only person who got along with you? Do not treat our daughter the way my family treated us."

It went silent. I heard my mom go into her room and start crying. I felt so torn, but I stayed with Amara.

I couldn't help but think about how different it would have been if Poowah Deepa and Divya were here. At this moment, I missed them so much and needed them to be here.

I cleaned Amara's face. We sat in silence. Our eyes spoke to one another.

We went to my room. She cried. I held her.

We fell asleep in each other's arms.

Leaving for Guyana

On the last day of school, we said bye to everyone and signed each other's yearbooks. The grade 12s were all crying. I don't know how Amara and Damian will make it work; she's going to McMaster for life sciences and he's going to the University of Toronto for engineering.

Serena asked if she could write in my yearbook. We met on the student council and bonded instantly. She is Filipino and loves soca, so it was an instant connection. She said her cousins are mixed with Trinidadian and they lived with her for a few years. Her uncle was always playing some type of soca music while he was fixing his car. She had pin-straight brown hair, down to her bum. She wasn't skinny, but she wasn't curvy— a nice in-between. I hope next year we hang out more; we have both been selected to be grade 10 reps together.

Naraine had my yearbook; he said he wanted to write a surprise. I still can't believe I'm dating him. I'm not sure if I'm his girlfriend; he hasn't asked me, but he calls me his girl, so maybe?

Amara and I couldn't stay at school long; we were leaving for Guyana that evening. I felt so excited to see everyone after years but super sad I wasn't getting to have my summer love with Naraine. We would be spending six weeks of our summer there. Our cousin Darshani was getting married and my mom's sister Mausi Baby, also known as Aunty Soma, was the youngest sister of my mom's siblings and her daughter was the first to be getting married from our first cousins. This was going to be a big fat Hindu wedding.

I saw Naraine before I left. We had finished writing in each other's yearbooks; he told me to read mine on the plane. I told him I would email him while I was away, depending on the internet.

He gave me six kisses on my cheek, one for each week I was going to be away— and one forehead kiss. I hugged him, and of course, smelled him and then let him go.

"Don't miss me too much," he shouted at me while I walked away.

I got home and it was rush, rush, rush trying to finish packing and getting ready with the awkward silence between my mom and Amara. They still hadn't spoken to each other since prom night, besides through me. I hated being in the middle of all this drama.

***

Dad dropped us at the airport. He gave me and Amara a kiss and hug and told us to listen to our mom and be good girls.

"Mujhe tumse pyaar hai."

He looked at my mom, "Seeta I will miss you, my dear."

Mom responded with an "Mmhmm."

They hugged and he kissed her on her forehead— one of the only times we've ever seen our parents be affectionate to each other.

We checked in, went through customs, and sat waiting at the gate. It wasn't like my mom and Amara to not talk to each other. Amara was my mom's favourite child, for sure. Whenever she was on the phone with Guyana, she only talks about Amara, how she is on the honour roll, and how she's working, and this and that. It sucked to be stuck in the middle and, to make matters worse, my dad was barely home so team Amara was just me and Amara.

Mom had been packing for weeks; sardines, Cheerios, chocolate, clothes, gifts, shoes, and housewares. Four out of the six suitcases were dedicated to bringing things to Guyana versus our clothes, but we'd be bringing back frozen fish and tons of fruit. Mom's big sister Didi stocks her up nicely. I looked out the window and watched the planes take off.

We all sat in silence.

"I want to meet the bai when we come home."

What just happened? Did she really say that? Amara and I looked at each other.

"Okay."

"I don't wan you leave fah school and we not talkin… I uh…"

She stumbled on her words and held back her tears, silent pause.

"I'm very proud of you Amara." Mom began getting teary-eyed, but she pulled it together and stopped talking.

Amara hugged our mom.

"Thank you, Ma."

Whatever my dad said to my mom clearly worked because who is this lady and how is she okay with Amara dating? I wonder if she will be okay with Naraine. I can hear her now saying, "dah bai nuh geh prapa pants fah wear?"

PA system: Flight 767 now boarding to Guyana, Georgetown.

We found our seats and sat on the plane. As much as I wanted to open the letter Naraine wrote for me in my yearbook, I didn't want my mom to see it, so I took my journal out. I decided to write to Divya.

Dear Divya,

So much has happened that I must tell you. I have no idea where to begin. Meh, geh one man gyal! Lol, you would laugh. I think he's meh man, but we haven't made anything official. We are "checking" or just "talking" with kissing? He hasn't asked me to be his girlfriend and I dunno if I should ask him. I still can't believe I'm dating him. He's so delicious and smells so good. I brought his cologne to Guyana so I could smell it every time I miss him. Yes, I know I'm weird! Anyhow, he wrote me a letter that I have yet to read because, well, I'm sitting beside my mom and Amara on de plane. Mom will want to macco and ask who write me a letter and I nah able geh into all ah dah after what went down between my mom and Amara. You won't believe what happened right before we came on the plane— my mom is open to meeting Damian! She and Amara haven't spoken for weeks since the whole prom incident went down, but I really think Daddy-Ji talking to her about his experience helped her be more open to Damian. Well, you know we love Damian because it's Damian— and he's just SO nice. He and Amara compliment each other so well. I look forward to seeing what happens when we get back!

The last month of school was great. I ended mediocre with all Bs in my subjects, nothing compared to smartie Amara, but I'd say it's a win given my learning disability. I wrote in Kristen's yearbook despite what Shantelle had to say. I hope I can patch things up with her over the summer. Maybe I'll bring her back a gift from Guyana. She always asks for sand from beaches whenever people go away. I think that would be a thoughtful gift. Maybe I'll get some from the seawall or 63 beach. I do miss her, I hope she can forgive me.

Girl, I belong to a friend group too. I've never had this before. It was always just Kristen, you and I. Now there are other people and I talk to so many different people. It's so cool. I wonder what grade 10 will be like? So many people wrote in my yearbook. I even have a photo of me and the girls standing up against the wall. I wouldn't say I'm popular, but I think I'm in the middle. It feels pretty awesome :)

I'm super excited about this wedding and seeing Nani. I love her back rubs and her tight hugs. She always smells like Vicks and limacol. Great Nani hasn't been doing well. Apparently, she has been bed-stricken. That lady is 95 years old, I wonder if I will live dah long. She keeps talking about her back-in-the-day stories according to Darshani and her sister Vena, maybe I should listen to them. I haven't seen our cousins in about four years. I wonder how everyone looks. I wonder how Darshani's future husband looks— if he's cute or not so cute. I know you always wanted to go to Guyana. You were Mom's fave— always chatting her up about Kaieteur Falls and asking her about her childhood in Guyana. Maybe that's why she liked you so much, you spent so much time with her.

I still can't believe I survived my first year of high school without you. We had so many plans. I do think about you and hope you know I haven't forgotten you. I miss laying in bed pretending to do our makeup because now I actually wear makeup, but only eyeliner and sometimes the mascara Mom lets me wear. And I miss watching movies with you, especially Indian ones. I miss doing each other's hair and practicing different braids on each other and going for walks with Poowah Deepa to the lake and buying ice cream. I miss you both so much. I wish things hadn't happened the way it did. I wish I could have done more. Ugh...

I have to go now. I don't want Mara and Mom to see me getting emotional, but I'll write about Naraine's letter when I get to Mausi Baby's house.

Until then.

Love you always,

Anju

Acknowledgements

Dear Divya was born in 2020 when Tiara Chutkhan put out a call for short stories. I wrote the story in five hours and sent it to her. I wasn't sure it was what she was looking for, but she said yes! I continued to work on it and it was published in *Two Times Removed*. I did not imagine the feedback that I received from folks, it was phenomenal. People asked if I was going to continue writing it, wanting to know more. I didn't think anything of it, but then I said to myself, why not continue the story? I have always tried to find creative ways to educate the next generation of Indo-Caribbean young people about their history, but also, when have you ever read about two brown skin girls who are not the typical description of main characters being the main characters of a book? When have you ever read and seen names that are familiar to you? I know for me when I was a young person I didn't. And so I continued to write and this book was created during long nights of nursing and having my youngest nap on me. I hope the story continues and we continue to learn more about Anjali and her journey through high school.

To Stephanie, thank you so much for going back and forth with me for months on the cover. You are a true artist and made my vision come to life.

To Tiara, thank you for believing in my story, for working together on editing this book and for being a part of this journey. I am so grateful to you.

To my mother and late father, thank you for doing your best in raising me, for providing me with all the opportunities you never had, for continuing to love your chutney, soca and Indian music, and for being proud of where you both came from.

To my mother-in-law and father-in-law, thank you for your continued support, your help with the boys, for always making us yummy home-cooked Caribbean food that we need to learn how to make, your patience, your kindness and love. You both created the best gift for me and I am forever grateful.

To my team of strong amazing supportive women. You all know who you are. I would not be here without you ladies, you are all ambitious, driven, focused, and I am so grateful that we continue to build each other up and grow together.

To my grandparents, whom I've never met, my grandparents who have left me, and my grandparent who is still here. I know my Aji and Nani never had these opportunities, they both were married at a young age, gave birth to nine children and dedicated their lives to their husbands and children. To be able to read and write is something that I hope you are smiling up above.

To Nekai and Nelin, my sons. Everything I do, I think about you two, your future, your connection to your culture, and understanding your history. I hope you enjoy this book one day and understand this was for you two.

To Neal, my husband, my life partner, there are not enough words that I could say how grateful I am to have you by my side throughout this journey we call life. Your patience and love and continued support in everything that I do is a true blessing. You are and will always be my best friend.

I hope you all enjoyed the book and stay tuned for grade 10.

About the Author

 **Saira Batasar-Johnie** locates herself as a brown, Indo-Caribbean Canadian cisgender woman of Indo-Caribbean/South Asian Indian descent. 1st generation settler in T'karonto/Toronto, Ontario situated on the territory of the Anishinaabe, Mississaugas of the New Credit and Haudenosaunee Peoples, with recognition to "The Dish With One Spoon" wampum and Treaty 13. Saira's parents were immigrants escaping violence, oppression and poverty in Guyana and Trinidad. Saira is a Child and Youth Care Worker as well as a mom, wife, daughter, sister and friend. Saira is passionate about bringing the history of Indo-Caribbeans to the newest diaspora of young people. She hopes to educate young people with her words and inspire them to continue their journey of understanding themselves in this world.

Connect further with Saira on
Instagram @saira.batasar.johnie
email s.batasar@gmail.com

About the Editor

Tiara Jade Chutkhan is a book blogger, writer and editor born and raised in Toronto. Through her platform, Tiara strives to promote diverse and culturally specific literature. Her blogging has allowed her the opportunity to review books for HarperCollins, Penguin Random House, Simon and Schuster and Dundurn Press.

Her work has been published in the Caribbean Camera, Brown Gyal Diary, Write Magazine, Caribbean Collective Magazine, and Brown Girl Magazine. Tiara is currently finishing a Creative Writing Certificate at the University of Toronto's School of Continuing Learning.

She currently has two books out: *Two Times Removed: An Anthology of Indo-Caribbean Fiction* and *Two Times Removed Volume II: An Anthology of Contemporary Indo-Caribbean Stories.*

About Illustrator

Stephanie Rambharos is a Toronto-based Indo-Caribbean multidisciplinary artist. Originally a traditional painter, Stephanie has honed her skill in graphic and digital design over the last 7 years. She has curated content and created pieces for networks like the Brown Gyal Diary and Dear Coloured Girl and continues to use her talent to capture the visions of those around her. Her work is often reflective of her journey of self-discovery through identity.

Until
Grade
10